ISBN 978-0-9983915-2-6

Design :
Magali Meunier & Sophie Heidenreich

Published by
MACKENZIE PRESS
14835 Sunny Lane
Orland Park, Illinois 60462

www.anancygeebook.com

Produced in France, Published in the United States,
Printed in China by Global PSD

To request a personalized copy or to schedule
a book signing/school reading, email
nancy@anancygeebook.com

a nancy gee book

Written by **Nancy Gee** · Illustrated by **M. Meunier & S. Heidenreich**

The Secret Room

Look into your secret room and discover your surprise!

Nancy Gee

MACKENZIE PRESS

Chicago

The Secret Room is dedicated to
my daughter Ellen, who reminds me
when I need a happy moment
to read the childhood book we shared.

Maddie goes, Kitty goes,
Where they go, nobody knows!

Up the hill they go,
Down the hill they go,
Every day they go,
But where do they go; nobody knows!

Up the stairs they go,
But what is this building; nobody knows!

There goes Dewey
into that room,
Maybe we should join him
very soon.
Every day he goes, but why?
Nobody knows!

Look what we see,
Look what we hear,

Reading stories; how fun is that,
Sharing with Maddie and Kitty Cat.

It's time to rest,

Then hurry back to hear the best!

Al and Sal, you followed us here,
Now bring your pals, come follow us there.
Join the children in the reading room
Hurry along, we'll see you soon.

Hi Dewey, what's behind that door?
We'll come later to explore.
We must hurry along to the reading room,
Must join the kids all so soon!

Here we are all to listen,
But wait; all the kids are missing!

Maybe we should go and look,
As they would never miss a book!

Where did the kids go?
It seems, nobody knows.
Oh let's explore this room next door

We can't believe our eyes,

It's Dewey the dog; what a surprise! The kids are reading to Dewey,
Now this is truly groovy!

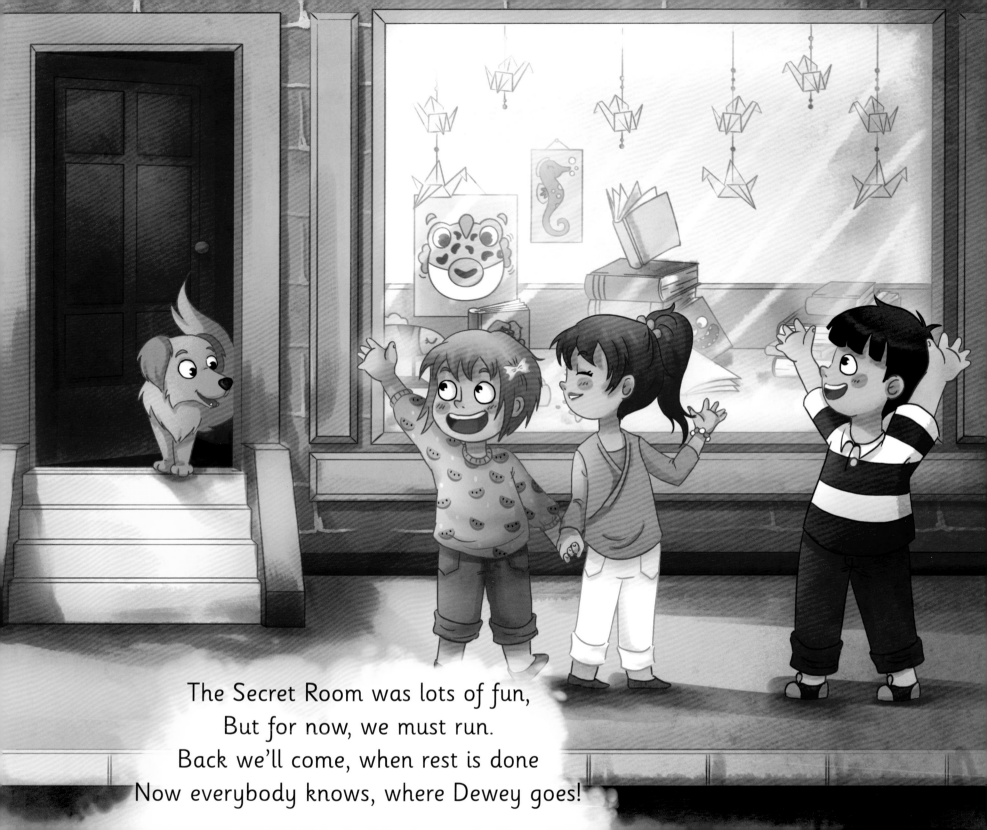

The Secret Room was lots of fun,
But for now, we must run.
Back we'll come, when rest is done
Now everybody knows, where Dewey goes!

Where you go; what you do,
Now everybody knows!
We all want to be like you,

Reading with kids, we can do!

Stop, stop at the Secret Room,
Dewey's surprise awaits you soon!

New friends have joined our Secret Room
We'll all read together very soon!

Reading raccoon,
you'll hear him soon.

Reading with Kitty,
who is oh, so witty.

Reading with turtle,
could make you chortle.

Reading with bunny,
is oh so funny,

Reading with flying squirrels
will make your head twirl!

Back we'll come to read
one- two- three- four And many more!
How fun was that?
With all the animals including Kitty Cat.

Author's note

The inspiration for this book came from my encounter with a R.E.A.D.® dog at a library where I was doing a reading to children from my Secret Book Series.

A dog entered the library and disappeared into a room. After my reading, my curiosity lead me to investigate. To my amazement, when I opened the door to the room where the dog had gone, there was a child on the floor reading a book to the dog whose paws were resting on the book and whose eyes were looking at the child with great interest.

From that moment, I decided to share the story behind this amazing program, which is called Reading Education Assistant Dogs (R.E.A.D.). R.E.A.D. animals are registered therapy animals who volunteer with their owners. R.E.A.D's mission is to improve the literacy skills of children with the assistance of registered therapy teams acting as literacy mentors.

 The R.E.A.D. program is the first and foremost program that utilises therapy animals to help kids improve their reading and communication skills and self confidence, and also teaches them to love books and reading. Intermountain Therapy Animals, R.E.A.D.'s parent organization, has focused on growing R.E.A.D. around the world since the program was launched in November of 1999 in Salt Lake City. Today, thousands of registered R.E.A.D. teams work throughout the United States, Canada, the United Kingdom, Europe, South Africa, Asia, and beyond.

Come read along and enjoy THE SECRET ROOM. Dogs giving to kids and kids giving to dogs.

READING EDUCATION
ASSISTANT DOGS®

A PROGRAM OF
INTERMOUNTAIN THERAPY ANIMALS

Nancy Gee's journey into writing started not long after an unknown animal got into her sock drawer, only to be discovered by the family cat. Her grandsons loved having her tell and retell that story, and challenged her to write a book.

"When I published 'The Secret Drawer', I knew this was the start of a new chapter in my life". The Secret book series with each book based on a true event has proved to be an enormous success both in the U.S. as well as internationally.

For more than thirty years, Nancy has owned and operated Maywood Industries, a wood fabrication company that sells industrial lumber and related building materials. Her entrepreneurial skills and drive have served her well in her publishing endeavours, as has her philanthropic work both with foundations as well as corporations. Nancy is a graduate of Drake University and lives in the Chicago area.

www.anancygeebook.com

Magali Meunier is a graphic designer and illustrator.
Sophie Heidenreich is an animator and illustrator.
Both live in Bordeaux, France and each have received their degrees from the the French visual communications school ECV.

www.magalimeunier.com
www.sophie-hei.tumblr.com